Me, Myself, and the Pandemic

Me, Myself, and the Pandemic

By

Vishnupriya Pillai

Kerala Publishers

Title: Me, Myself, and the Pandemic

Written by: Vishnupriya Pillai

ISBN: 978-81-948932-4-0

Kerala Publishers
Manacadu, Trivandrum, Kerala, India – 695009
publish@keralapublishers.com
www.keralapublishers.com

Online and Distribution Partners: Amazon, Flipkart, Notionpress, and DC Books

Printer: Akshara Offset, Trivandrum, India
First Printing, October 2021

Pen by: Vishnupriya Pillai
Illustrations and Cover by: Accent Premedia
Copy Editing and Typeset by: Accent Premedia
Website: www.accentpremedia.com

Dedication

This book is dedicated to all the teachers and classmates of Grade 3N and 4N (2019–2021) of Our Own English High School, Dubai

About the Book

This is a book written by a 10-year-old spontaneous little girl. The pandemic took a heavy toll on adults, teenagers, kids, and it didn't leave anyone behind.

When the first announcement of online school came out, like every student out there, she was delighted! Because she had something to preoccupy her hand and mind during the pandemic. But as time went on, her crown of excitement turned into a frown of sorrow... She realized the best time of her life was when she was in school (except the studying part obviously). Whispers throughout the hall during the break, snickers which turned into smiles that lit up the classroom, all those reminiscences mesmerized her. So, she started jotting down all the best memories in school and thus this book was born.

This book portrays the real-life characters that a 10-year-old interacted with. She tweaked the characters to evoke the interest of the readers, but the inspiration is from her real school life.

A journey through the mind of a 10-year-old and her perspective of the fellow beings...

Contents

CHAPTER 1

Introduction

Hi, I am Vishnupriya Pillai, a fourth-grade schoolgirl. My parents call me a 'restless being' as I take rest only while sleeping. I cannot sit idle at a place for more than thirty seconds. This is the reason why I got the nickname 'Wrecker ball'.

My elder sister is Sivapriya Pillai, an eighth grader, blessed with a handful of friends who supported her in everything. She is like a 'Goody Two Shoes', who ruins your life as she gets everything she wants, the fame, the popularity and is always pretty hyped while I am just the opposite.

My father is a gentleman with an overgrown moustache, a scintillating smile, and a whimsical sense of humour. He is a kind of cheapo and loves to get stuffs for free, and a manager by profession.

My mother is a short woman with bright eyes and an interesting smile. She is an entrepreneur and anchor by profession. She has many more jobs like cooking, cleaning, gardening, shouting at me, making sure that I am always studying, and many more.

She is the one who has this idea of making me write this diary, saying that if I concentrate on writing my feelings, I will learn new vocabulary and new experiences. I am journaling my thoughts down only because I can get my mother off my tail and pass the time. Do not expect me to go on, Dear Diary this, Dear Diary that. Dear Diary, this happened. No!

I am just planning to talk to you like you are my best friend. Well! Like a friend, as I don't know much about you; so, let us get started.

My parents are mostly on the same page. Only on ridiculous things, they do have arguments, not even on simple things.

However, once there was a big dispute. It all started when my father thought about buying a particular not because this car was too glossy and polished, giant and had lots of space.

No, it is all because 'it was on sale'.

Above all, it does not have space to fit a family of four. It only had two seats.

So, my mom got crossed over by my father's foolishness. She believed that the family should stick together and experience everything. Therefore, he was forced to return it. But this argument did not end there. This is the line she regularly uses to win any argument against my dad; if my father bought the wrong food, she immediately comments, "see, you are always looking for promotions, even for the car'. In a nutshell, she basically wins every single argument.

WELL! IT ISN'T AS BAD AS THE CAR THAT YOU BOUGHT LAST TIME

My father is very innocent and naïve. So, in arguments, my mother takes up instantly. If you do anything out of the line, she will immediately give her punishment like grounding. No, she does not believe in grounding. She won't even make you clean the house either, but studying is her basic punishment. She is very strict and has a new body pain every single day. She will drop that into the conversation when she is not in a mood to talk. However, she is not bad enough to stop giving us food. Instead, she will cut off the TV limit, comes early from her work to make sure that we are immersed in studies, stuff like that.

My father is way too different; every time think hard about his punishment, and right when you do not expect, he will say, "you know this happened because of this". He tried to match it with unrelated things such as, if he sees you in a bruise, he will comment, "It is because you are watching too much TV".

He would compare it with the silliest things. So, you could say my family is weird. Maybe your family is weird too.

In this diary, I am planning to share with you some of the interesting incidents I came across, the lessons I learned, my thoughts, and my imaginations. I presume the readers can correlate these incidents with their own school days. I had changed the real names of the characters to protect their privacy. Certain incidents were exaggerated to increase the pace of the narration.

I would like to start with one of my earlier memories.

CHAPTER 2

A true friend and the lesson I learned

I was very shy, introverted, and had no friends when I was in grade one. I used to sit in the corner of my classroom without getting noticed by anyone.

There was only one person who tried to speak with me, Vihana. But I believed she was so mean and over smart for her own good and tried to ignore her.

One day my teacher was discussing the features of onions; the topic was quite interesting to me. Moreover, I knew a fact about Onions. With all the courage I could, I asked ma'am,

"Ma'am, Can I share a fact about Onions?"

Not only Ma'am but the entire class looked at me in astonishment!

Ma'am got happy and delighted as I finally spoke up.

She grinned delightfully, "yes, please proceed".

With my hands shaking, legs shivering, and lips trembling, I somehow shared the fact with my classmates.

I noticed Ma'am's smile was slowly fading away.

"That's not correct", boomed the teacher raising her eyebrows.

With a heavy heart, I went back to my seat, trying to hold back my tears.

Vihana, feeling pity for me or rather empathize with me, suddenly stood up and whispered something to the teacher's ear.

Ma'am called out my name with a pleasant smile and said, "Vishnu darling, you are correct, but that is about baby onions".

Within no time, I found myself standing in the middle of the class with a big, fat star on my forehead, stuck by my teacher as a token of appreciation.

I was overwhelmed with emotions and felt like I was over the moon.

That moment I realized Vihana was indeed a true friend, and I should not judge anyone without getting to know them.

"Empathy is seeing with the eyes of another, listening with the ears of another and feeling with the heart of another"

—Alfred Adler

"EMPATHY IS SEEING WITH THE EYES OF ANOTHER,
LISTENING WITH THE EARS OF ANOTHER
AND FEELING WITH THE HEART OF ANOTHER"

THIS WILL BE PERFECT FOR YOUR BOOK

(I bagged first prize in interclass Just A Minute Grand Finale for sharing this incident)

CHAPTER 3

Perspective always matters...

Think of the meanest teacher you ever had. I bet you have thought of plenty.

For me personally, she was my grade 3 teacher.

I felt like she was so proud of herself as she got so many awards and never took a single leave in her 20 plus years of career. Once, she literally chided one student in the class, "I have never raised my hands ever to my students, and I feel like I have to break that record".

She enjoys doing annoying things and once asked, "Raise your hands if you don't like me".

A lot of us were shy to admit that we didn't. But one person had the courage to raise his hand and said, "I want to be honest".

The teacher replied, "I don't care, and I respect myself". (Now I know what she said is correct, self-respect is a much-needed virtue)

I always feel that she is too bossy. She constantly shouted at me as I had bad handwriting (even though I understand it's for my own good), which irritated me (not only she almost all my teachers).

One day I went to school dressed up as the scientist, Thomas Alva Edison. To get more originality and to be realistic, I wore a wig. I looked hideous. On the bus and in the school, everyone stared at me as if I were an alien, and I could imagine most of them snickering as I passed by. I ran to the class and burst into tears.

To my surprise, Ma'am tried to comfort me by saying, "They don't know what they are talking about. You be you, those who laughed at you are jealous of you because they can't pull of you and don't have the courage to be like you" and only because of her motivation I was able to perform my part well in the assembly.

Another time I enrolled for a science project. With the help of my uncle and aunty, I made a rain harvesting project. But the teacher-in-charge rejected my project, citing that I failed to explain the project well and ripped me off. But ma'am noticed how sad I was, convinced the teacher and she let me in as long as I prepare the speech well. She called my mother and told her that "I know Vishnupriya is capable, and I don't want to ruin her self-confidence. So, I went to meet the teacher-in-charge and promised her that I take that responsibility".

She made sure that I byheart my speech well. In addition to that, she put an effort to call my home even on Friday to verify herself that I prepared it well.

I moved to that school in that academic year only and didn't have any friends, and the new school was less pampering than my old school. I missed Millennium and my besties so much.

I started pulling my hair out in the class, and I felt it was satisfying. I used to wrap my finger around the hair and pull it. When ma'am noticed a lot of hair strands near my chair, table and inside my book, she thought that I had a severe hair fall and immediately contacted my mother and instructed her to take care of my hair by giving a coconut oil rubbing.

But my mom got frightened as she could not find out hair strands at home and had taken me to the hospital, and the doctor found out that I had done this when I got stressed and rectified it. If she didn't find out my issues and get them corrected, I would have continued this habit for the rest of my life.

By the way, we are Astro twins. It's a pleasant feeling to wear your birthday caps with your class teacher.

Even though how strict a teacher can be, there is still something inside them that will shine out in the deepest and dark times to help you out. I can genuinely say that she is the one who supported me the most in my 6-year-long schooling.

Small things she had done for me is kind of had a big impact on my life. I owe her a lot.

"The influence of a good teacher can never be erased".

CHAPTER 4

The particular type of drummer

In my old school, I used to have a music teacher. She was young and super-encouraging. It was around that time I started learning drums. I was proud of myself and told Ma'am about the things I learned. I was expecting she would call me saying, "We will teach the class how to play the drums together", which never happened.

However, I do remember one specific memory which I keep close to my heart.

She wants us to relate xylophone to drums. "I may need a specific drummer for this", looking at me, she stated. Immediately I stood in front of the class.

Around five people started complaining and whining, "Ma'am, I also know how to play the drums".

Ma'am ward off that by saying, "She is a particular type of drummer. Isn't she?"

Embarrassed, I blurted out some blabbers, which is the only thing I knew about drums. I guess that was completely wrong. Maybe out of pure sympathy or empathy, with a smile, she said I was so close to the answer and asked the class to clap for me. She gave me a tiny little sticker, but instead of putting violently on my forehead like the other teachers, she kept that on my palm and from that moment onwards, I ran around and kept showing that to everyone. My sister didn't think it was that special, but my mom thought it was all worth it.

"What the teacher is, is more important than what she teaches".

—Karl Meninger

CHAPTER 5

It's all because of a photoshoot

If you have crooked teeth, do not smile ...that is my policy.

But sometimes, there are tight spots where you must, and there is no way of going back.

I was supposed to take some photos, with my brand-new dress for my mother's boutique, **Nilofer Collections**. While we were taking the photos, I tried to smile without showing my teeth, as I was embarrassed.

My mother's smile turned into a crooked grin, by seeing me posing without smiling.

"Why don't you show your teeth?" Mom threw her question as expected.

I murmured, "My teeth look like a disaster, my Incisors are crooked, while my Canines are like crocodile teeth. I'm too ashamed to show them off".

By noticing my gloomy face and watery eyes, Mom suggested, "Why don't we go to the dentist?" [ok, see, this is a great idea because a dentist will help you, but it may take at least a year]

In my head, I thought, "Dentist", with those sharp pointy utensils and a screwdriver, will go into my mouth!

NO!!!!, I was not going to take that risk of becoming the dentist's lab experiment. [what I scared, come on! they point sharp objects to my face.]

I rejected my mother's idea with a straight and commanding voice, "Absolutely NO".

Days passed by, and my sister had her photoshoot. She was nicely showing off her gleamy white teeth with no crooked ends!

I went to the mirror, all sad, as I did not have perfect teeth like my sissy, and even worse, a permanent tooth (canine) is growing in the same place as the milk tooth. I guess I had to do something. I couldn't bear it any longer, and I would even be a lab experiment at this rate.

I vividly remember that time at the Interschool Lego Competition, when my team bagged first place.

We got an opportunity to rub shoulders with our principal for taking a group photo to publish in the yearbook. While we were clicking the photos, I didn't smile as usual.

The principal enquired, "Why don't you smile, Vishnu? You seem to be worried; what happened, dear?"

I answered with a sheepish smile, "I don't have any teeth to show".

The principal, plus a few of my friends were started laughing loudly, as if I cracked a joke. I felt like I was draining all my emotions into a bucket.

I heard my mother praising my sister for being a born model; that's when I snapped back to reality. I felt gloomy, so I marched up there and called out to my mom,

"I am ready to go to the dentist; under one condition, my smile should become perfect".

As my father liked my confidence, he booked an appointment with the dentist, who just happened to be my fathers' friend.

I got scared that my gums were going to be ground into shreds.

The next day, I was ready to face whatever disasters I might face when I meet the Dentist. I wore something stylish to make me feel confident.

I reached the clinic with many thoughts like, "Maybe I should not have come, I can smile without braces, I am not sacrificing my gums".

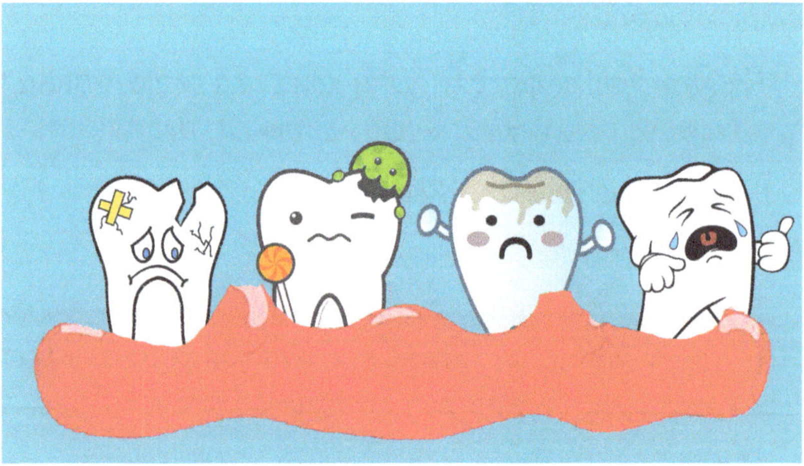

That's when I got called out.

My nervousness quickly turned into a fright. Within no time, I was lying on the medical bed surrounded by machines, quaked, and quivered.

The dentist, George Uncle, appeared and flashed a charming smile. After had a thorough check-up, he whispered to us the strategy.

"We plan to remove the milk tooth to give the canine ample space to grow and put braces to turn it".

I gulped and asked, "What are we going to be doing today?"

He murmured, "Nothing at all".

I was relieved and lay there keeping my fingers crossed for the finest.

He then instructed me just to open my mouth once again, and within a fraction of a second, my tooth was in his hands.

I got admired by his quick movements and professionalism, but I am still going to wonder how that helps to make my teeth not crooked.

I just wish to say this, go to a dentist so that you can have some great teeth which will help you when you plan to click a snap, or you might even become more popular with those perfect teeth, who knows...

"A smile raises your face value".

—Anonymous

CHAPTER 6

A terrible mistake

[mainly my mother's but whatever]

Yes! You heard it right. I have made a terrible mistake in my life. You might be thinking, "Oh! Did you get detention? Did you get expelled from school?"

No!

It is even worse than that. You could not even imagine what it is...

I committed a mistake by choosing my mother tongue 'Malayalam' as my second language. You might be wondering, "seriously? something as minor as that?" I will explain to you.

Not only Malayalam has trillions of letters, but those joined one another, making more complex letters. Kind of trippy? Just wait! There is more. Most of the letters merge with themselves and make a double-decker letter!

In addition to that, they also interconnect with other random letters and convert them into some alien letters. Not only that, these letters may link with different chihnams, on the left, right, top, bottom or even in the middle to make new letters.

Sometimes there are words that look and sound the same but have a different meanings. Furthermore, when two or more words are joining together, some of the letters disappear! Plus, as a bonus, they are all impossible to pronounce. So, let us all scream it together 1, 2, 3 Malayalam is impossible...

MALAYALAM IS IMPOSSIBLE

To make my views more believable, I checked a thousand different sites and all of them simply agreed with me.

Even Google admits, "Malayalam is the most difficult Indian language. It is both difficult to learn and speak as compared to any other language in India. It might be the second toughest language in the world after Chinese".

So, guys, studying Malayalam is like rehearsing tongue twisters every day and even every moment of your life!

CHAPTER 7

The outbreak

You might be asking what outbreak? Well! If you were born yesterday, then it might make sense to me that you don't know about Covid 19. The rest of us already know about it and hate it even more than you might know. Well, I will explain it to you.

Once upon a time, there lived a man who ate a bat [Yes, I know it is weird, but wait!]. It gets so much worse, and this bat ate a rotten apple [I don't know if this apple had some disease or something but must have been strong] and without knowing that the man had it and got infected, this ignoramus mingled with all his friends, went to different countries and spread the coronavirus, short-form Covid 19.

The world went to lockdown; in other words, we were locked within the four walls of our room. Now many people must stay in quarantine.

Don't know what it means? Don't worry, and most fellows heard about that word for the first time only after the outbreak.

Now every single being has to wear a mask and gloves to be extra safe; squeeze a nice bottle of hand sanitiser in your back pocket.

CHAPTER 8

The era of online classes

When the world went to lockdown, the school literally came to our home.

Welcome to online class [No, you are not goanna be welcomed properly] Now be ready for a bumpy ride and a discoverization [yes, I know it is not a real word] of bad and good apples.

As your mentor, I am planning to give you firsthand information about online classes, both the bad and good. The online class is indeed a rollercoaster ride, but it's worth experiencing once in a lifetime.

The best part about an online class is that you can wake up late and all you need to do is log in at the last moment.

You can also be as messy as you want, as all you need to say is that your camera is not working.

But you should not forget about the bad side, and not everything is sunshine and rainbows,

First, your mike can get unmute by mistake at the least expected time, and your parents may utter something stupid, and there goes your reputation. So online classes can be tough as well.

CHAPTER 9

No!!!! I am not picking out juicy fruits

In onsite class, there is nothing juicy [that is only one of the reasons why students hate school, by the way]. Our secrets are not revealed much. But during online classes, we can figure out the real people and the fake ones. The juicy secrets are just spilt when you are in your home habitat, as we act like our normal selves. We had seen the true colours and personalities of many. Lives of everyone. Yes, it was not much interactive, still some of us added some spice to the class, including me.

So do not get too comfy when you're at home.

So, this is a survival guide not only about online classes but also about real life.

Let me familiarize you with some of the distinctive characters in my class. I bet all of you can relate.

Victoria

The ultimate nerd, most popular, smart and organized, fully respected, and never utter a wrong answer in her school life. A favourite disciple of all the teachers except Malayalam teacher for obvious reasons [She is not in Malayalam class as her second language is Hindi].

Definition of perfection, if you ask me if she is bad at anything or has any weaknesses. I would rather spell it than say it... N... O... T... H... I... N... G...

I doubt whether she is aware of her full strength. I bet (a promise I will be putting inside a locker) she will be voted to student council when there will be only girls, and she is going to open her mouth in wide, woooooooooooo!!!!!!

She never got embarrassed in front of our class.

There is a three-kilometres-long list of what she is good at! And one and a half millimetre of things she is bad at.

Freddy

He is super smart and like a brainiac 5 from Super Girl. As he is aware that he is smart enough and hence treat all of us like little babies.

I am terrible at singing, but he is the opposite, blessed with a melodious voice. Once I sang in the online music period with a shaking voice, Freddy looked at me, pushing his glasses to his forehead and showed a thumbs up as if "You are doing a good job! continue little baby!" to instil a little bit of confidence in me. Don't try to give me a mollycoddle treatment, dude!

However, if you ask me the weirdest thing he had done, it is probably this. The trash can in our class was full as someone brought a whole McDonald's bag to school. Freddy needs to put trash in due to some reason or the other.

"Uhhhhh, there is no space here", he exclaimed!

Instead of throwing that to the next nearby one like everyone else, he pulled up his sleeves violently, as if he was going to hammer down some bad guys, started to push all the trash down by compressing it with his bare hands. After he did, he looked at us as if he owned a feather in his cap and bragged.

"Look, all down!"

And toasted his lunch like a football player. He missed it, unfortunately! And the entire trash bounced back.

But it was kind of cool! I was impressed!

"Dude, you are a smart cookie".

Later he washed his hands and declared,

"I am all clean now, and I am a genius".

And started walking down proudly against the corridor walls, spotted five trash cans that weren't full, which he could have easily thrown his garbage in, acted like he hadn't seen them at all and marched pompously towards the farthest. I guess this incident represents him. 'A proud guy'.

Najma

She is the leader of the girls, always appears cool, with full of energy. A mixture of nerd and popular, she balances both in a perfect blend!

Very focused on her academics, she can effortlessly switch between sophisticated to colloquial accent, while speaking with teachers and her classmates.

Sneha

Well! She is like me, a person who wants to answer all questions, a person who always get ignored by Ma'am, a person who is always ready for everything and a person who thinks that everyone out there is her best friend.

She does everything with a passion unlike me, which I cannot explain in words.

Raj Singal

What do I say about him? He behaves like everyone else is under his control. The class is for him, who can unmute his mike at any time, speak and show us whatever he wants.

One day during reflection time, unmuting his mike, he started whining, "Ma'am, I feel so bored". At the same time, we were all trying hard to figure out what to play. With a frigid spinner in one hand, he started shouting 1...2...3...go.

Super-duper angry I, shrieked, yelled, howled at the top of my voice, "Raj, mute your mike at this instinct".

He shot an irritated look at me and winced at the disgust in my voice. Poor Ma'am muted him, and nevertheless, he was smart enough to unmute himself. Left with no choice, Ma'am muted the entire class!

He is one of the curious characters whom I encountered in my life. While we were in grade 3, I was assigned with monitor duties for a small period. I must write down the names of people who chitchat, on the blackboard. I decided to write the full names as there are persons with the same first name. I wrote his name as 'Raj Single.'

He marched towards me, all agitated, "Hello, my parents are Single for you?"

Apparently, it turned out that his last name was 'Singal.'

Another time while I was looking for my headband in the cupboard, which is kept in front of the school, displaying lost and found items. I turned around as I had a feeling that someone was looking at me; my intuitions seemed to be correct. My eyes met with two suspicious eyes; it was none other than Raj. He looked me up and down with contempt and questioned me.

"Are you stealing stuff from the locker?" I replied sternly, "Excuse me, and I am not stealing anything".

I guess he didn't believe me at all and followed me till my bus. I was freaked out and zoomed off to my bus mates.

Benoy

I couldn't figure out, the first time I ever spoke to Binoy, who Riitu is obsessed with.

The boy who is least interested in academics is the most popular guy among boys. He is a chubby boy who somehow gets everyone's attention.

Onetime while in grade 3, during break time, Raj whispered something in Benoy's ears, and he giggled and screamed, 'Vishnupriya… Vishnupriya…'. Overhearing my name, I enquired,

"What?"

Raj stammered, "not now, not now", and tried to close Benoy's mouth as if he was trying to suffocate him.

Poor Benoy pleaded, "Leave me; I am not saying anything".

Later out of curiosity, and to quell my anxiety, I asked Benoy, "what it was? "He replied, "you were out of line".

I wondered, "for that, you have created this much drama, dude!"

I am still suspicious, "Was he saying something bad about me? 'Vishnupriya looks like a Halloween something'.

Binoy was not good at keeping secrets. But one time when it is about me, he can keep the secret! That's not fair, dude.

So Benoy fell into the list of people whom Neythan can't talk to. It is not because Benoy's character was bad. I would talk to him if he were the last person on earth... just that he is my friend, but not a best friend; rather, I would call him as my acquaintance.

During the online class, he doesn't make an appearance. The only time he opened his mouth was during the reflection period. He just turned out to be a rebel right now.

Neythan

Neythan is a person who prefers to be with the girls. I would rather say a popular boy who only talks to girls. We girls just ruled over him like he is our little puppy. Neythan is such a rhyming word, and we used to call him,

Hello, Neythan, the nerd.

Neythan, the naughty.

He tried his level best to assign nicknames to us girls but failed miserably.

When he tried to address me as Vishu, I immediately protested, citing that' "Vishu' is a festival in Kerala. I can't possibly be a festival".

Only during field trips, he has permission to sit with his once best friend Benoy or to do whatever he wants. I guess, only during field trips, he had got justice.

He is a mathematical genius who is going to be the next Einstein.

Malar

Malar is a girl who is not that much popular. I often get confused with Malar and Sadia. She is smart and has some problems here and there. An ardent lover of technology, she may grow up to be a hacker one day!

Mathew Olson

Mathew Olson is obsessed with planes, and he tries to divert all our conversations to his own interests, **THE AIRCRAFTS**; the whole class knew about this. When we learned about that in Social Science Class, he was paying so much attention like "Yes, this is my subject".

"Dude, I hope to see you soaring in the sky!"

Noora

A popular gossip girl who is obsessed with fashion and whom I like much. You may wonder how far gossiping can go for a third-grader. It went on like this...

I really think that Victoria is trying to show off!

Who and who is lying so much...?

Dear, I wish to catch you at the next met gala.

Sameera

Only reason I came to know about her existence was that we both are neck to neck roll numbers. She and Mohdin made the whole class believe that they were cousins, but it turned out that they were not cousins, not even neighbours.

She is a good dancer, with luxurious long hair and has the capacity and audacity to comb such a long hair till her thigh and a next-level gossiper and a busybody.

"Noora is not attentive in class".

"You know Rita and Reetha hate each other, and they are fake best friends".

"I doubt boys are sharing a secret".

"I think Raj secretly hiding his last name, and I don't think it is Singal".

Where did you get all these ideas, dear? I used to wonder!

Aroma

A beginner in Arabic, she thinks that I am good at Arabic. She used to approach me to clarify her doubts in Arabic while I myself was struggling hard.

Whenever she approaches me with her queries, I am like,

"Where is the ppt? where is my Arabic translator?"

One time, during the Arabic exam, she asked me if I could be her translator? Then why are you writing the Arabic exam, dear? Go and write your English exam.

A super-duper smart girl and with down to earth attitude, she is blessed lucky enough to be on everyone's favourite list. While she was in India, she constantly had internet issues. Once she mistakenly unmuted her mike, and there was hubbub and noise, which distracted the entire class. We heard howling of wind, rustling, and crackling of leaves and branches—the honking of vehicles and clucking of chickens.

She herself tried to mute her mike but in vain. Ma'am tried, but that didn't work out either. We wasted one entire period trying hard to mute her mike.

A word of advice... Sit inside your house Aroma, not outside. We don't want to hear pigs and chickens squawking.

Neelima

Her passion is fashion and science. She is a quiet, shy but smart kid who doesn't want to show it off. I hope to see her as a researcher in science soon.

In my previous school, there was so much drama. But in a new school, everyone seems to be equal even though sometimes girls rule over boys. Everyone was friendly and jovial except **Aloe** and **Lana**, who were distant from me. Lana spoke with me a few times, and she seems to be an innocent and lovely girl.

Aloe maintained a social distancing from me even before the covid pandemic hit. I guess I am invisible to her.

One day Ma'am made me sit with her, and she directly told to my face, "Vishnupriya, it is not that I hate you, I just don't like you. You are too over smart, and you answer before your turn".

I bet all my friends and teachers agree with that statement except Victoria only because she is so nice.

Ma'am wants me to sit there to have an eye on her as she is weak in math. Math is one of my weak subjects. In that case, she must be bad at math's for me to assist her. she improved a lot over time; however, we never got a chance to patch up our differences.

Some people are like a banana that never goes rotten. But guys, that's not good. A plain banana that is always ripe and never gets rotten may always leave something inside your mouth. We need to find some bad side of them, as the law of the universe suggests that a good side always need a bad side to balance both. Otherwise, it is incomplete [yes, I am your moral science teacher, and this book is educational].

CHAPTER 10

The most memorable moment

I stared at the screen glued to my chair with no one to my right, and the only person in my left was my mom. She was just practising her pity speech for me, I guess. My sissy was in another room attending her class and clueless about what was happening to me. My father was in office, just thinking of what was going to happen or thinking nothing of me at all.

And me sweating in buckets while my eyes trying to open, my nose itching and I wanted to sneeze, my hair is looking as stiff as a rock and my lips so Chappy, I should have applied lip balm, but I forgot.

I was clearing my mind to get it prepared for the loser's speech, rewinding about all the challenging interviews and group discussions I had gone through.

Memories flashed through my mind like a movie.

I joined this prestigious school in the last academic year as a grade 3 student. The school is so huge and vast with over 10,000 students; literally, a GPS is very well required to locate my class.

One day, while I was exploring my new school, I accidentally entered the middle school session. A girl with a badge came up to me with so much attitude. She looked at me back and forth, judging me and declared.

"You don't look like you are in middle school".

I replied, "I am not".

She snatched my id card without my permission and asked me to report to my class; otherwise, she would report me to the supervisor.

I snapped back, "You don't have the authority to do that".

She beamed with a smug smile, "I do, I am a prefect".

I had never heard anything like that before. Therefore, I guessed it as 'Perfect'.

I wondered, "No one is perfect in this world".

As I had no intention for an argument, I fled the scene.

Back in the class, I discussed this incident with my new friends. They corrected me by explaining that they are 'Prefects', the leaders, and they are assigned with lots of powers.

I enquired them, "How can I become a prefect?"

They replied in chorus, "You should be good in both academics and non-academic activities".

That's when I decided that I would strive to become a 'prefect' in the next academic year. I wanted to test myself, build my confidence and self-esteem and gain new experiences by taking up challenging responsibilities.

I enrolled for all extracurricular activities in which I had the slightest interest and performed well to the best of my abilities.

But many of my seniors warned me that becoming a prefect is not that much easy as I think. Moreover, this year, due to the pandemic, there are no prefects, only head girl and head boy. Naturally, competition is quite tough, and my chances are slim.

I came back to reality and started preparing for my loser's speech.

Then I heard a sound rumbling in my ears,

"Vishnupriya"

At first, I could not trust my ears.

Ma'am repeated.

"The Head Girl of Primary is Vishnupriya Pillai, Many Congratulations!"

I got elevated to cloud nine by an invisible force.

Oh My God, I aimed for a prefect post, but you blessed me with the title of head girl; all my hard work has truly paid off.

14th September 2020, a day which I can never be forgotten.

The most exciting and memorable day of my life so far...

Due to the new normal, there were only 10 key positions in this academic year. I was lucky enough to be one among them.

Thus, my fellow nine student leaders and I became the first of its kind to take the responsibilities digitally. Yes! We are part of history now!

I strongly believe what Paulo Coelho pointed out "And you want something, all the universe conspires in helping you to achieve it".

CHAPTER 11

How I got the title of VIP

During my second grade, I showed no interest in anything that my Arabic Ma'am teaches. I don't like to answer any of the questions either. One time I encountered an awkward situation where my best friends were answering smartly while I was sitting there as if I was deaf and dumb.

Therefore, once I raised my hand, assuming that anyway teacher was not going to pick me. But to my horror, she did, and I blabbered some nonsense and got ashamed in front of the entire class.

In third grade, I got shifted to Our Own English High School Dubai. While the new students giving the self-introduction, my Arabic ma'am enquired curiously, "You are from Millennium? That is such a great school" I got noticed, and she always threw questions on me, and I tried to answer to the best of my abilities. She encouraged me to answer more which inculcated self-assurance in me. I had a feeling deep inside, "I am smart" It was fun too, as I was not in a position to attend beginner level like other new admissions; I felt like smartie pants.

When I climbed the stairs and finally reached the fourth grade.

I realized that there is no 'P' in Arabic, and pronouncing my name was an uphill task to my Arabic teachers. Ironically my name has two P's. Vishnu Priya Pillai. My third grade Arabic ma'am preferred to call me as 'Vishnu' My fourth grade Arabic ma'am could not pronounce my name either. I suggested to address me as 'VP'. She misheard it as 'VIP'.

She mockingly teased me, "Oh! You are a Very Important Person now".

And continued to address me as VIP and started to callout my name quite often, which encouraged me to be super attentive in class, and I improved substantially.

During the last day of class, she told me, "Next grade onwards, whom I will call as VIP". A million memories swirled around the head. I felt so sad and emotional after hearing such a thoughtful gesture from ma'am.

Mathew Olson intervened, "ma'am, at least girls can see you; we never get a chance to meet you as we are moving to boys' school".

Pin drop silence! We didn't get a chance to meet our boys and bid a proper farewell; we all felt so gloomy.

She is such a great guru because if someone gets anything wrong, she never put them in the spotlight or make fun of them or roast them, unlike most of the other teachers. Instead, she asks someone else to answer and continue. Even though she was aware that some of us were using google translator, she smiled and continued her teaching. I strongly feel that she has lots of so-called 'teacherly qualities' and is certainly an incredible guru.

CHAPTER 12

Majid ate the Eiffel Tower

One day, during Arabic class, Mohdin kept on flying his hands in the air.

"Ma'am, can I say? ma'am, can Mohdin answer?"

Ma'am allowed him to speak at last.

"Well, Mohdin, what is the answer?" she inquired inquisitively.

Ma'am, لفيا جرب لكي دجام [for those who do not know Arabic it means 'Majid ate the Eifel tower'.].

Ma'am did a slow clapping, and she stated with a smirk, "Majid ate Eiffel tower?"

I bet you that everyone was shrieking their hearts out, keeping their mike muted. [He was supposed to say Majid ate al hares, an Arabic food].

CHAPTER 13

Mr. Roast

[No! I am neither talking about roasted chicken nor about beef]

In an online class, there is always a superior guy who thinks he is the second teacher, and for us, it is Mathew Olson. Never try to obey him as that's what he wants. Instead, you should just ignore him and let your English teacher deal with him. Well, he acts like he is superior to everyone, including the teachers, just because he is 10 years old, just one year elder than all of us, his classmates.

He always wanted to answer in class even though he doesn't have any clue about it and a word of advice for everyone! "Don't raise your hand if you do not know the answer".

[well, come one! if you don't know the answer, don't pretend as if you know it. Use your brain, dude.]

Mathew is determined to destroy Raj Singal's life. He is somewhat anti-Raj. One day during PE period, Raj switched on his camera and sat there with both his legs crossed and hands at the back of his chair and staring at everyone as if he was the teacher.

Raj can't raise his hands and legs at the same time. "Oh, No, no, no Why did we expect him to behave like a normal human being?"

I called out his name, "Raj", and he seemed to be very glad that he was getting all the attention, so he responded enthusiastically, "Yes",

"Why are you switching on your camera if you are not interested in doing any exercises?", I asked.

He joked mockingly, "Because my neck is paining".

Another word of advice: Do not give lame excuses. If you are going to make an excuse, make it a good one, at least. He just gave away Mathew a new topic to roast him.

"Then you can exercise with your hands and legs". Ma'am intrigued.

"Raj, it's very bad and started explaining about the importance of exercises".

Mathew warned, "Raj, wait and see what your body will be turning into; you will be fatter than everyone else in the class".

At last, purposely with his mike in unmute position, Raj grumbled awkwardly,

"Ha, I got over with my PE class".

Ma'am got utterly offended and looked at him like she would turn him into a tiny ball and throw him into the sea.

His blatant behaviour made the entire class go silent.

CHAPTER 14

Doesn't my laptop crave for a bath?

There are many stupid things that I did in my life, but I am going to name the most annoying incident.

Once I was attending English class and noticed how dirty my laptop was as it was literally a dust bin with oil, water, and food stains. An idea buzzed in the back of my head. Without a second thought, I have given my laptop a nice bath with water and soap.

I guess my laptop didn't like that at all, and well, it stopped working. That's when my dumb head realized that adding soap to a laptop is very toxic. So guys, Don't act like a stupid as I did myself.

CHAPTER 15

The mysterious Roaster

She is a soup with six spoons of spicy masala, one-and-a-half tablespoons of salt with a lot of roasted beef and a handful of peppermint. She is a blend of sweet, salt and roast. She has a firm voice. Even though she seems funny at times, she always has a roast in hand. As she never turns on her camera and seems rather mysterious. I can only imagine from a tiny circle of a picture of how she looked the year before. She might have changed, so I tried to perceive all the abbreviations of how her look would be. She might have long hair, dark blue or mining eyes. Her choice of vocabulary is out of the box and so quite catching to me.

Please lock it in.

Keep it firm to the heart.

Instead of saying 'byheart', she prefers to say, "Lock it in your heart".

I am sure you all will agree with me, there will be a teacher in every grade who is strict and asks all these thought-provoking questions and, in my class, she is none other than My English teacher

So, you have to look out for these teachers as they might call your name at any time. You should either 100% know the answer, or you must have a good enough trick for her to think you have a problem. If she doubts that someone is not paying attention, she will keep on asking the question until they get it wrong, and she will start repeating, "I knew it! I knew you were not paying attention".

No one can ever win a fight with My English teacher; she always wins every battle, so do not try to go on a battle with her even though you are prepared because you are not.

Before, when I was not thinking straight at all, I thought I could beat her in a battle.

I asked stupidly, "Ma'am, I said the same thing as Victoria", and my ma'am answered with an angry snarl, "No, Victoria was straight to the point, you weren't".

"But ma'am, I still stated the correct answer", I murmured sheepishly.

Pin drop silence on the other end.

She has already won the battle. At the same time, she is very mysterious and humorous, and a part-time roaster too.

She loves roasting people, so if you are one of her victims, either zoom off the meeting immediately or divert the embarrassment to someone else. One time she sarcastically responded to one of the students who asked a silly question.

"Oh, Mason, you just woke up! Such a surprise! Can anyone tell him 'The Case of the Candy Bandit' is a grammar topic or a literature topic?"

Well, to sum it up, my English teacher is a part-time roaster, the queen of asking questions and the winner of all deliberations.

CHAPTER 16

When you have not studied for a quiz, expect this

We have all been in the situations like this, when we have not studied for a quiz. But when the teacher notices that, it just goes down the hill so fast. I will share with you a time in which my classmates went through the exact same thing.

One day in English Period, our teacher made lots of quizzes in Nearpod. Each of them was all about comparative degrees. She was checking the marks and assessing. She kept on shouting at many people about how they made silly mistakes, then she suddenly turned her head in slow motion, peered at an answer for a while and then squealed with the top of her lungs.

"Mathew Olson, you got everything wrong from first to last! I explained three times, and especially for the last one week, still you do not know, you need a stick".

I guess, Mathew decided not to respond. Ma'am called him many times, and I perceived intrusive in the hope of making everyone chuckle, "Maybe he went to find a stick". But mam did not laugh. She just nodded her head which I failed to guess, was of agreement or disagreement. She proceeded to check everyone's paper and revealed their remarks.

She posted another quiz after that, but unfortunately, again, Mathew got everything wrong except one. She got furious. She was soundless, and that was not a good sign, now. If a person got even one question wrong, her head would explode, then she gave a 5-hour rebuke about how important this grammar topic is and how much pain and effort she puts into guiding us; with extreme trepidation, the period somehow finished.

There was one more period on the same day, Ma'am looked as calm and serene as always, but then, of course, Mathew destroyed it. This time she just gave a quiz with two questions. She took a deep breath and sent the quiz, and within minutes, she broke down because Mathew got both questions wrong. she yelled, "Mathew, you need a stick six times a day from now on".

Well, Mathew got it hard, so I am going to warn you if you are in a situation like this, do not do inky pinky punky. Instead, listen to the teacher or even ask a friend if you have any doubt. Just do not sit there terrified, ok.

CHAPTER 17

How many sections are there in a sentence?

Let me share with you another incident. One day at the end of the class, to sum up, everything we have learned till then, my English teacher asked,

"How many sections a sentence is divided into?"

Everyone shrieked, "two".

But I holed even louder, "three".

My ma'am immediately responded, "Who is that clever one who said three?"

I retorted softly, "Ma'am Vishnupriya", and I am like, "Ma'am, I thought about considering the object as well".

She just gave me a warning nod and continued.

Thank God she seemed to have in a good mood; otherwise, she would have stretched her arms through the screens and clutched my ears and drawn it out and asked me to leave immediately. I guess she will press the button herself and leave.

I bet if it was in onsite class, she would have been stricter, and she would make us to stand near the board at least.

If she had done that with Mathew Olson, the scene would have been different ...I still remember once he forgot to bring his English book, and our teacher made him stand near the board. But instead of feeling sad or crying as a normal student would, he thought he was that mature and started laughing, and eventually, the whole class joined hands with him. So, it turned out to be a terrible mistake.

Let me warn you if you are not sure about the answer, please do not unmute your mike.

CHAPTER 18

May I leave?

With an over smart brain, I had a weird habit of answering questions to everyone in the class, acting like the teacher does not exist. Most of the teachers do not bother about it or ignore me or intervene unless I blurt out some Himalayan blunders.

One day in the midst of that, a rumbling sound fell in my ears.

"Oh Vishnupriya, you are the teacher. I am so sorry, I didn't mean to disturb you, I may leave, you, please continue".

I wanted to run so badly; my feet were glued to the floor. My mouth felt dry. I wished to say sorry, but I could not open my mouth, as if they were stitched together with some invisible thread.

I got embarrassed, and my parents would be called, who had already warned me several times about being too over smart and doing things on the teacher's behalf.

I may even get expelled from the school. My mind got filled with nightmares! My face turned pale, and my heart turned inside out.

Again, the same sound....

"So, may I leave Vishnupriya?"

Finally, with so much effort, I apologized for my mistake and promised, I would never repeat it. Till now I rue the day.

I learned in a hard way; I should never answer on the teacher's behalf. It is the teacher's job, not mine.

My English teacher is one of the interesting things that happened in my life.

CHAPTER 19

Sometimes you can be a little bit pragmatic

Many times, I have been the dullest person in the room, and I am not going to let you be the dullest person in the room too because then there is no meaning to this book. So, let's get on with the story.

One day during science class, I kept on shouting at the top of my lungs, "Ma'am Vishnupriya acknowledges, can Vishnupriya say?" Ma'am, let me answer the question.

The question was, "if the population of frogs decrease in the given food chain, what will happen to the population of snakes if the snake's prey is frogs?"

I responded quickly, "the population of snakes will increase".

My logic was that since the snakes don't have anything to eat, they will be more fit and energetic, and they can move around freely... Even though everyone's mike was muted, I bet they were all rolling on the floor hysterically laughing. Everyone screamed, "Noooo".

Well, you cannot accuse me of being a little more pragmatic.

CHAPTER 20

I am lost

I was in my grade 3 science class. At the end of a chapter, Ma'am was asking questions. For the first question, I raised my hand. She said, "No Vishnupriya", and pointed to one of my classmates who said it wrong. Ignoring me, she asked the same question to 10 more people until she got the correct answer.

She moved to the next question, and I kept on raising my hands. The same thing repeated for the entire worksheet, and my hand was getting soar. Finally, for the last question, I lowered my hand as I was clueless.

Immediately I heard my name being called out, "Vishnupriya".

In my head, I felt like, "Excuse me, you did not let me answer any of the questions; immediately after I lowered my hand, you have a piece for me?

I blabbered some nonsense.

"Vishnupriya, you are not paying attention in class? Teacher exclaimed.

I am lost.

VISHNU YOU ARE NOT ATTENTIVE

CHAPTER 21

Reliving the past

I have a lot of topics about my English teacher, but I never talked about my last English teacher, she was exceptional too. She is like my mother but a bit nicer and funnier. She has the same habit as my mother. When she is happy, she's the greatest person on earth put on, but when she's in a bad mood, she can be a demon and be very Savage.

So, let us have an incident where she turned out as a Savage demon. It was the middle of an English class. Ma'am was not in a good mood as it was a long day, and it was scorching outside. Only one thing is needed to make her completely angry.

As always, Mathew is the one to trigger this. He forgot to bring his notebook, third time in a row. His excuse was bad, and he tried explaining, "ma'am, I misremembered it. I thought we did not have English class today".

Ma'am was not satisfied by that response, as she knew every day, we had an English class, so she could not possibly think why he had forgotten.

Ma'am got so furious, and she made him sit outside the class and take his diary, and then after class she made him write down,

"I will always remember to bring my book",

and of course, he forgot the very next day but let's save that story for another day.

Now let me talk about the times when she behaved like an amusing Unicorn who brings flowers to everyone's hearts. This time she was in jovial mood as she cleared an examination with flying colors. She was smiling the entire time. plus, she allowed us to do fun activities which I fancied notably. She also offered us candy every time we got the right answer. So, I always pray that she should stay in a felicitous mood every day. She is my cherished teacher because not only is she entertaining but she also loves me and treats me like her second daughter that she never had. I longed for her to be my English teacher for 4th grade.

CHAPTER 22

Exploring the milky way

In Malayalam class I never had the courage to answer. But one day it just came to me to raise my hand. I still wonder, why, as I didn't know the answer. Either because I wanted to prove myself that I deserve the golden badge which is kept at the corner of the room, or it is because I wanted to show others that I am worthy of it. Either way I did raise my hand. Ma'am called out my name. It seems like no one else raised their hand, since it was the hardest question, it was one of the hot questions in a foreign language, which I don't know how to even pronounce. I just stammered, barely even saying a word in this tongue twisting language. My teacher immediately realized what is going on. So, she stopped for a second and asked me if I wanted to pass.

I still wanted to prove myself, I jabbered some random things in Malayalam which made zero sense.

Teacher interjected, enough! Pass!

Everyone started laughing and got an idea about my proficiency in Malayalam.

I pledged myself, "I will be learning hard" I learned a little bit by the next day enough to know my lefts and rights. The following day in the class, I was not that bad; I was able to answer a question without stuttering. Well, it may not seem like much to others, to me it was like exploring the entire milky way in one day!

Ma'am started clapping as if I am a baby!

I longed to say, "Ma'am, please don't clap for me!" But I kept quiet.

Do you know why?

In Malayalam class, we are allowed to speak only Malayalam, and I don't know how to say that in Malayalam.

CHAPTER 23

The onetime teacher got over smarted

During summer in India, how hot it is... The question goes to Benoy, but he fails to give a proper answer.

Ma'am commented, "You don't know the climate of your home habitat?"

"Ma'am, but I never have been in India during summertime. I used to visit India during monsoon season".

Benoy smartly fought back. That makes a lot of sense, dude.

CHAPTER 24

The Yellow Bus, big and loud

On every bus, there will be a second Principal sitting in the front. They won't let us speak, they won't let us move, they won't let us change our place, they won't let us to eat, they won't let us to sit with whom we want.

On my bus, that person is my bus aunty.

She always says, "Shhhhhhhhhhhhh!

Vishnupriya, why do you always make so much noise in the front?"

One day out of nowhere, she announced, "I am going to move you to the back."

She may have thought that moving me to the back was a brilliant idea. She may have a false perception that if I sat near my sister, she might have kept an eye on me. But my sister didn't care at all. She was busy with her own gang.

Bus aunty made me sit with a girl who seemed to be my sissy's age; to her left sat a 6th grader.

Both waved their hands.

I am the one who actually initiated the conversation(just saying), but they were not hesitant to say' hiiii.

Later, we found something in common. Not all were that great, but we did find out that we both love certain cape pop groups dramas. We instantly bonded. Her name is Shahida, a 9th grader.

On the way back home, she sat with her best friend Anjana, and I sat behind her seat, staring at them and envying their bonding.

From behind, I try my level best to intrude in their conversation, as I fear being left out. (FOMO... The Fear of Missing Out). As soon as Anjana leaves, she is left out with no other choice than sit with me. It is rather I make sure that she sits with me.

We had a good time together. Yes!

Is it a trial story? Maybe!

One day on our way back home, she narrated one of the interesting incidents which happened in her class.

She got scared when her history teacher bobbed up in a substitution period. Surprisingly the first thing she ever asked was,

"Does anyone know what BTS is?"

Everyone got happy to know that she turned into a cool teacher! The entire class raised their hands unanimously.

This time the luck favoured Shahida as the teacher picked her.

The teacher asked, "How many members are there in BTS?"

She responded within a fraction of a second with full enthusiasm and pride.

"Seven"

"Which country started World War two?" The teacher went on...

Shahida froze!

Yaaaa...

She stood there rooted to the ground and wiped sweats from her forehead with a shaking hand.

Without uttering a word, Shahida stared at the emptiness.

"People here know how many members are in BTS and even their daily routine. But clueless about what I was teaching for the last one week!"

The teacher couldn't comprehend why they were so inattentive in her class!

CHAPTER 25

A couch potato when I am around

If you have an older sister, be glad that you have a role model right in front of you. Even if she is kind or rude, you still want to be like her. When I was in fourth grade, I wanted to be exactly like my sister. She has so many pals, and she is so close to all of them. While my sister has sleepovers, private moments, and outings with them, I am trapped in the corner of my room with no real friends but only fictional characters in storybooks.

She already has a lot of different people with whom she stands. Do you know what a stand is? Well, stand basically means you are biased with someone, or you like them as an idol. You got it, right? She discovered Cape Pop, ..., NIT, and told me all about them. Now I am obsessed with Cape Pop. She got obsessed with K Dramas and me too. It is like whatever your older sister does, and you wish to do too.

She has a bunch of different types of pens, pencils, rubbers and sketch pens and everything you ever want, and simply you are not at the correct age to have them.

However, there are some downsides too. You always get whammy down by her. If you have two sisters, it is cool, and you will get only a few of them. But if you have two siblings and you are a younger sibling, you are doomed. You get everything, which is old; it might be musty, crusty, or even may have blood stains and cracks on it. Since my sister has amazing taste, I used to get the best things ever.

As a voracious reader and a bibliophile, my sister has a virtuous collection of books, which you may wish to read. When you do, you just fanned your life.

She may ask you for a glass of water or a charger, which is right next to her because she suddenly turned to be lazy and lethargic, whenever you are around, which is quite annoying.

If you are lucky enough to have an older sister, whoof!!!!

CHAPTER 26

When the lies backfired

It was our family time, and my sissy and I were cracking jokes intensively. One of her classmates, who was smart and always punctual, came late for the class and everyone got surprised as she had never done so before. When Ma'am enquired, she murmured..." I am so sorry Ma'am, I overslept".

In a delightful voice and with a pleasing face Ma'am responded, "Thank you so much, Shreya, for telling the truth. Everyone should be like Shreya. Don't blabber lies like, "Ma'am, I didn't see the link. Any way Shreya, don't repeat this".

Before I could control my laugh, imagining how many would be coming late in the coming days, citing so many truths, my dad cracked another one, and the story goes like this.

In his childhood, they were going for a field trip from school, and one of his friends arrived late by half an hour than the stipulated time. When the teacher in charge interrogated him, he said he had severe stomach pain. One of his friends backed him up. What happened next is a part of history, he was banned from drinking juices and eating junk food, and the poor fellow helplessly watched his fellow mates enjoying all those dream dishes. His own tongue backfired him. I couldn't help laughing for the rest of the day.

CHAPTER 27

Why can't I have my own phone?

Everyone asked me why I needed a phone?

Excuse me; you are not my mother, so I don't need to keep answering all your queries, but anyway I will...

First and foremost, I need to set my alarm even though I never wake up to them; still, why not give it a try?

I need a phone to listen to music, even though I don't like music

I need a phone to watch exercise videos, even if I have never exercised in my life.

I need to play games even though I don't know how to install them.

There are so many reasons, even though I am running out of reasons to list out.

But the thing is I need a phone so that I look cool. I guess I have already given pretty many explanations. [wink... wink...]

CHAPTER 28

I am in shape guys

I hate when people comment I am out of shape. I am a flat square 2 D shape. Isn't that a shape? So, I am not out of shape. I am 'in shape.'

Don't imagine me as a skinny, slender stick with a smiley face on it. That's not how I look like. Even though, most people interpret me in that way. I am a small stick with a very tiny face, it's not because I am malnutritional, but as all the food I eat directly transported to my legs. They are gigantic, obese, and powerful. My hands seem to be like noodle strings. My hair is as long as Rapunzel's. My cheeks are as droopy as Dumbo's ears; my eyes are pitch black on normal days. When on sunny days, it is similar to emerald hazelnuts.

Does it fit perfectly like a puzzle, or is it still missing one piece?

CHAPTER 29

Are your hairs in place?

When I have scrolled through my school pictures, I frequently felt low. My hairs are not in place, so I know the tension of not blinking or looking good.

I am going to tell you how I look glamorous in photos. I first started off by making a very tight pony, so it does not fall off your head and ruin the look. Since makeup isn't allowed, I just put on a light powder and facial cream. I ironed my clothes over 62 times to make them look professional. I shampooed my hair the day before and put whole other stuff for the hair, which I don't even know how to pronounce, like shampoo and conditioner for straightening and glowing; rose conditioner with scent booster and many more to be added to the list.

CHAPTER 30

How beautiful I am...

My forehead may be bulgy, and I may look like a stick, my nose may be crooked, and I may look like Draco Malfoy of harry potter, my cheeks may be small, my lips may be as thin as a paper, I may have a unibrow and my face shape maybe like a triangle, but I feel like I am beautiful just like the way I am. Only when you compare yourself with others, you may feel ugly. You should be your role model, and you should try to figure out your characteristics, personality. Everyone is unique in their own special way.

CHAPTER 31

Online classes in nutshell

During the lockdown days, I was left with uncertainty. The pandemic turned my world upside down. Locked inside the four walls of my house with no one to talk to other than my parents and sister, I felt emotionally drained. I was never aware of the existence of the zoom, clueless about Pinterest and Netflix. The worse part was that I didn't have the contact number of my friends. My dance and instrumental classes met an abrupt end. Left with no choice, I read all the books in my home library 300 [it is actually 1009756342785] times, but I thought that was too hard to read.

That's when the online classes started as a beacon of hope. Still, I was apprehensive about the outcome of screen learning as I craved to meet my friends and teachers face to face. To my surprise, online learning bought so much fun along with it, I must admit. During onsite classes, Ma'am dictates notes, and we write those down, or we do experiments or go to ICT labs.

During e-learning, teachers used so many interesting apps, which made learning so much exciting, thrilling and enjoyable. They taught us with the help of PowerPoint presentations, Class kicks, near pods, quizzes and fun games, which made us feel competitive to learn everything. We got a feeling that we were going to ace each subject. Together we did exercise, together we danced, together we sung our favourite songs, together we played, together we went for a super cool digital tour, when we felt so nostalgic, teachers drove us through the memory lane of our classrooms, seats, and corridors. We participated in online competitions like the English Elocution Competition, Math's and Science Olympiad, Read Run Competition, Sudoku, reusing of one-litre plastic bottle challenges if I name a few and bagged e-certificates and e-medals.

Some of us picked up a chance to participate in experiential learning projects and got first-hand knowledge about the art of preparation of chocolate tiramisu. The teaching faculty did a commendable job and are indeed the real superheroes in our life.

They acted like we were in a real classroom, behaved as if nothing ever happened. So, all of us felt super-duper comfortable. The energy and inspiration we got from our teachers in these unprecedented times were incomparable. We did enjoy the online journey more than we expected. I wish to salute all the hard-working teachers, supervisors who stood as pillars of strength and the unsung supporting staff who tried to help us to get adapted to this new normal. Together they led a smooth transition from face-to-face to black-screen learning, which we experienced less steep and more impressive and satisfying.

A big Thank You to all of you from the bottom of my heart.

During the summer vacation, the school provided us with free access to an online book creating app. The first-ever book I made was through this app. It was super amusing as it looked exactly like normal books but with fewer paper cuts. It motivated me to create more and more books with short stories, poems, and book reviews. In that year itself, in November 2020, I became an author by publishing my book of poems, **'VISHNULOKA_MY WORLD OF WORDS'** in Sharjah International Bookfair. It was one of the good things that happened to me in lockdown days.

I wish to share a few short stories I did write in **'write reader'** with you all...

CHAPTER 32

The Cloud Carter

Once upon a time, far away in the land of the clouds, lived a naughty and empathetic cloud, named Carter, who belonged to the nimbostratus group. He was fluffy, Rey and liked to float in the sky. He always travelled together with his parents, friends, and relatives as a 'billow of clouds'.

Once they were drifting towards a rainy area, cloud Carter trailed behind, and he got separated from his family as he took a wrong turn. Little cloud Carter got scared. He worried that he would cry out a wrong acid instead of rain without the companion of adults!

So, he set off in search of his fellow clouds. On his quest, he came across a swift westerly wind and asked him politely, "Dear, will you please tell me where the rainy season had already begun".

The wind replied, "Yes, far away near the Himalayan mountains and the Indian Ocean, there is a country named India, you can go there".

He thanked the cloud and continued his quest to the Asian continent.

On the way to India, he got stuck in air traffic as a flock of tiny birds were crossing, and it took a long time to clear the route.

To make matters worse, the trees were arguing over some silly matters and wouldn't let anyone pass through. After the matter was solved and when he finally reached India, the monsoon had already finished.

He was so sad but did not give up. He wandered around and asked a towering tree, "Will you please tell me where the rainy season just started?" The tree answered after a while, "In Costa Rica, the rainy season has already begun., dear child, you can go there".

The little cloud Carter thanked the tree and continued his quest to the North American continent.

While he was scampering, a person stopped him saying that he needed a visa to cross between the Indian and American continents. Since he was just a cloudlet, he didn't have a visa, and the visa process has taken a long time! And when he finally reached Costa Rica, the rainy season had already finished, and summer began.

The cloud couldn't bear it any longer and lost all hope, and he then decided to float aimlessly. He wandered through the countries and continents, seas and oceans, hills and valleys and mountains and deserts.

While resting at the top of the Sahara Desert in the African continent, he shared all his miseries to the sand, who appeared to be very sympathetic. The sand smiled and suggested, "Why don't you improve this desert by turning it into greenness? Third times a charm, right?"

Even though he knew that to make that wonder happen, he had to cry profusely, he agreed. He cried all over the sand for four continuous nights even though it hurt him miserably. And on the fifth day, he woke up with an amazing sight. Small sprouts of seedlings were dancing in the breeze.

He immediately sensed; all his hard work was going to pay off!

After a few months, the desert became a land with a variety of plants bearing fruits. Colourful flowers bloomed with delight. Butterflies and honeybees fluttered over the streams, which rushed out from deep inside the sand. Within no time, people moved into this paradise from all over the world. The cloud felt proud of himself, knowing that he had become the reason for a new civilization.

Moral...

You can achieve anything if you put your heart into it...

(I bagged second prize in an online storytelling competition by narrating this story)

CHAPTER 33

The ridiculous fight

One day during break time in a small classroom, a Pen sat with a Pencil.

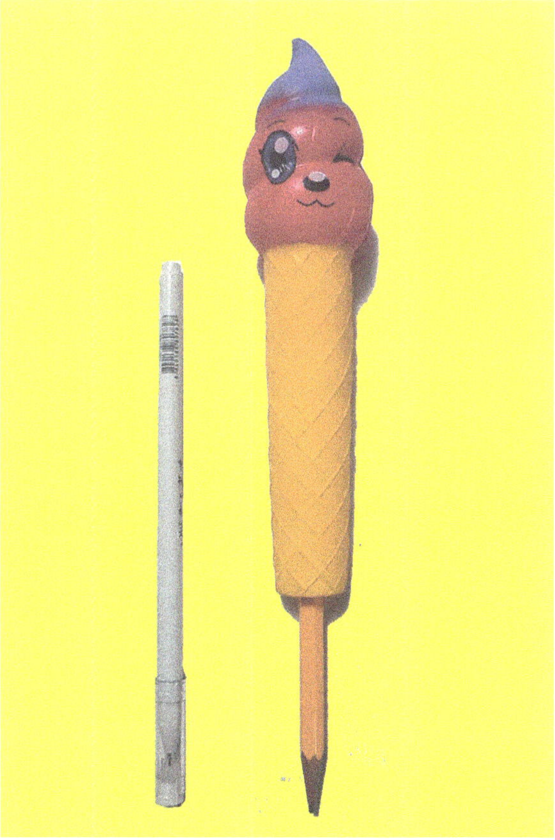

They were fighting over something ridiculous.

"I am better than you as I am more environment friendly", said the Pencil to the Pen.

"What is the use? Even a small child can break you!", Pen rasped.

"I am the first pal of a child", Pencil exclaimed.

"That's just to improve their penmanship", Pen fought back.

"I let my owner rub out their mistakes, while your owner doesn't have that choice", lashed out the Pencil.

"My marks are permanent, but your marks may fade over time", Pen snapped back.

"I have a crown known widely as a cap, so I am royal unlike you", Pen announced with a laugh and added, "I am more expensive than you".

Hearing this, the Pencil stood rooted to the ground with a pouting face.

"I can write and draw pictures", Pencil stormed after a while.

"Well, you always go through tremendous pain to get sharpened while I just have to refill my tank", Pen screamed with a cackle.

"That pain makes me sharper and neater", Pencil fought back with a grin.

"That is pretty cool" Pen was amazed.

"Thanks, and you are too", replied Pencil with a smile.

"Well, my friend, you have such a long life span. But I keep on getting sharpened and will die eventually while you can just refill your tank", said Pencil with a smirk. Hearing this, the Pen felt so sorry for his bestie, Pencil.

They do agree that both of them have good and bad qualities like all other creatures on earth. Still, they are unique in their own way.

Morale...

Always remember that you are absolutely unique, just like everyone else.

So don't compare yourself with others and always be yourself!

CHAPTER 34

The wheel of life

In the suburbs of the amazon forest, the sun was at its highest point. The leaves were rustling and crackling in the cool breeze, and the flock of birds were warbling their melodic tune in symphony.

In sync, an army of ants marched downhill with crumbs of food on their head. When they almost reached the anthill, an anteater bobbed up and stumbled on the clearing, and it reached its snout inside the anthill. Accidently anthill fell with a big halt, a pause and tilted to the right and collapsed.

Millions of ants crawled out of the collapsed anthill in a rush. But before they could escape, a group of anteaters emerged from the bushes and gulped them all with their sticky tongue.

This incident is known as the wheel of life, declared uncle Kalong to his spellbound audience, a candle of young anteaters.

The children exclaimed, "Wow, cool".

"With this, today's lesson is over", Uncle Kalong winded up.

The parents held children by one hand and cradled them while swinging through different branches till they reached their savanna.

Back home, after having a delicious lunch of ants and termites, the smartie Pan curled up to rest, with its huge tail covering both his head and body.

At the same time, his brother was on his way back home after a tiresome day. A Jaguar pounced on him from the back. It tried to fight back fiercely with its sharp claws, but Jaguar being stronger and healthier, killed the anteater. Once the deed was done, the Jaguar, with its teeth, grabbed and dragged its prey to its cave.

Once done resting, little Pan and his mother tried to search for Pan's bro but failed miserably. They fell into a deep chamber of sorrow. The youngest of all, little Pan could barely eat, sleep or play.

Uncle Kamlong took the baby, cradled him on his lap and asked if he could narrate him a story. And so, he began sharing a long tale.

There was once a boy, who always ate any ant or termite which stood in his way even if he was not hungry. The God above realized, "IF PEOPLE LIKE THIS ANT EATER EXISTS, ALL DIFFERENT SPECIES WILL GO EXTINCT DAY BY DAY". The God almighty knew he had to find a way to kill that anteater to begin this quest.

He created an elephant to kill anteaters. However, when the elephant went near the anteater, he appeared big. He had a long trunk that could strangle the anteater and sharp tusks which could tear the ant eaters' flesh, and lastly, humongous legs which could quash an anteater, but the elephant was more interested in the grass behind him.

God grunted and then created a bear. The bear was strong and healthy. He had sharp claws to tear flesh and was an excellent fighter, but he ignored the anteater and jumped in the sea to grab fish and climbed the tree in search of honey.

As a final straw, God created a jaguar, who has a strong defence mechanism on its sleeve. As the name itself suggest, 'he can kill its enemy with one leap.'

This big cat, with its neck of packed muscles and paws bigger than the boxing gloves, can stroll up behind us, especially when we are unaware of their presence. We can also swing back with our ridiculously sharp and powerful claws. Victory may not always be on our side like in this story it was the Jaguar who had the luck to bear the crown of victory. Sometimes we may lose the battle. We have to accept those as the 'law of nature.'

God kept on creating more and more animals to complete this chain and called it 'the food chain' or, as we call it, 'the wheel of life.'

Uncle Kamlong groaned,

"See Pan, everyone has to die someday; that's how life works".

Uncle Kamlong's words made john realize even though his favourite brother died, he fought back like a ferocious warrior till the last breath of his life.

CHAPTER 35

Why I support onsite class

Many people asked me,

"Why did you support onsite class? You have to wake up so early, stay alone on your seat and in the classroom with no one beside you to your left or right in this covid pandemic".

Well, my answer is,

During the online class, there is a particular sensation that distracts me all the time, like every noise, every blender, every phone call.

Whenever I am staring at the screen and trying to concentrate, notifications of my favourite shows start popping off out of nowhere, and it's so tempting, and it triggers my curiosity levels, and I develop a fear of missing out. Then I will eagerly be waiting for the classes over without paying much attention to what the teacher is saying. While I am planning the schedule in my head, Ma'am is already done with the chapter, and I got lost midway.

Then my sister starts talking to her friends, and I have a strong urge to catch what she is saying and try to comment sheepishly...

The doorbell rings, and I am curious to know who is at the doorstep. Exactly at the same moment, Ma'am asks me a question. Alas! I was not paying attention and was left clueless.

While I was enjoying a delicious brunch, Ma'am threw a question to me out of nowhere, and I will start to blabber some nonsense, which is enough to spoil my entire reputation.

When it becomes a routine.

You don't mind it at all.

But once you are forced to go back.

You won't be able to adapt.

CHAPTER 36

Concentration is the key to success

This is a poem penned by me about what happens in online classes (everyone who has attended online classes may have experienced the same at least once)

I switched on my laptop;
And joined online class;
After pledging myself;
'Concentration is the key to success'.

While I was trying hard to do justice to my pledge;
The bell rang;
It went on ding dong ding dong;
I was waiting for my mom to answer the door;
Squirming and staring intensively at the door;
She is nowhere to be seen;
Wondering whether elves took her;
I muted the class and ran to the front door;

But as I opened the door.
I sensed my mom back of me with a long face;
Yelling and screaming to attend the class.
I sat back down and recited my pledge for the time of second.

Then the mixer went wild;
Sizzled and drizzled all over the counter;
Birr boom burr and buzz;
I focused my mind while muttering;
It is so hard to be diligent with such noise pollution around me.

As the time slips away;
The land phone started ringing with a hissing and clicking sound;
This time, I hold my urge to pick it up;
Having one eye fixed on the phone;
While another on the screen;
Until my sister attended the call;
She roared as loud as a bear;
Piquing my curiosity;

I eavesdropped on their chit chat;
listening intently to every blip and blabber;
Gossips and outstrips;
Enjoying every bit.

'Vishnu' I heard an echo with one ear;
Are you paying attention?
I stared at the screen with a dramatic pause;
And my quizzical expression conjoined with a death pan expression.

Answering the question with manipulation;
Mumbling and blurting;
I am lost, my reputation is shattered;
all my curiosity has taken a roundabout;
And turned into a puff of smoke.
After being humiliated before the entire class;
I kept my head low and tried to pay attention.

But next time, next time;
When I stare back at that screen, I can concentrate;
So, when you battle with online classes;

that concentration you can't seem to find;
Just wear a noise cancellation headphones;
As I did myself.

CHAPTER 37

I strongly support co-ed

I was trying hard to remember a new curious incident, which may trigger your interest. Sadly, I couldn't recollect anything. I am in 5th grade right now. That means no boys. They were all shifted to the boy's school.

When boys were around, they ran around the halls, corridors created lots of hubbubs, doing stupid things purposely to make us laugh. They have lots of energy in them, which make it boisterous to be in the class. It's not only about energy but the way they crack jokes. I am not saying that girls are not fun enough, but their humour sense is hilarious, and the positive energy they radiated can never be replaced by a tomboy. That's exactly why I cannot think of any more interesting incident.

I miss my guy friends and strongly support co-ed.

CHAPTER 38

Vishnuuuuuu

I am not sure if it is only for me, but I feel like whenever a specific teacher likes us or favours us, always have an affectionate, vocalized version of our name. For me, it goes like 'Vishnuuuuuu or Vishnooooo'.

That makes us remind ourselves about them. You may be wondering why all these suddenly came from.

Well! We had a visitor today!

An exceptional soul came to our class to meet all of us.

I felt so embraced. At first, I didn't even recognize her, and I just thought she might be a friend of our teacher, suddenly she called out my name, 'Vishnoooo'.

Hearing that sound, a million memories flashed through my mind. Within seconds I reached from point A to B.

I am so familiar with that voice; I can recognize that voice even in a deep sleep. My grade4 class teacher! (Who taught and guided us through online platforms and never met us in person).

She was such an encouraging teacher; even if we made a silly mistake, she didn't make a big fuss about it; instead, she tried to envelop that and tried to make us realize our mistakes.

"Wow......Vishnu proud of you!"

"Many more to come"

"You are a shining star"

"Pursue your dreams and reach for the star! You can do it"

These are just a few inspiring words she has said to me. Her positivity and encouragement brightened my days. She celebrated all my accomplishments along with me and made me feel like I am indeed a 'super star'.

Even in the hardest situation, she maintains a calm and composed posture "this situation is going to pass", that's her attitude. That's the entire reason why we all love her. Ma'am, I thank you for your patience, positive influence, motivation and much more!

I just want you, and I appreciate for a second all the teachers who have emboldened us, shaped us and moulded us into the people we are right now.

Author's note

I want to be flat out for you all... It was not even in my wildest dreams that I would publish a book. Let alone two books. My first book was a compilation of 70 poems carved by me during lockdown days which I have inscribed out of boredom. Impressed, my parents combined that into a book. When I entered the stage in the Sharjah International Book Festival to release it, everyone's eyes were on me. I felt like I was getting so much attention, and I liked and had enjoyed it to the fullest. I was informed that I was the youngest author in that year, which I have taken as a sheer surprise.

So many dignitaries came forward to congratulate me, clapping their hands, encouraging, and appreciating me, "Wow! Good job". TV channels have taken my interviews. It was another world. I got carried away and astonished by the responses.

In the end, Sharjah Indian Association President, Shri. E.P. Johnson, made me to promise that next year, i.e., 2021, I should come forward with an even more amazing book, which will blow everyone away. Ever since that day, I was like, I must finish what he had asked me to do, or I would be the worst person on earth. That motivates me to pen down this book.

Other than that, it was my friends in online classes, as each day, they were bringing something new to the table, showing their own colours, making it so fun and dramatic during these pandemic times. It's literally written all over their face, "write about me!" I may have chosen things a bit, or I may have exaggerated.

I take this opportunity to thank the authorities behind the innovative idea of online classes and the faculty of Our Own English High School, Dubai, who made that into effect, without which the book would not have been born.

I am grateful and impressed with Mr Mohan Kumar, the external affairs executive at Sharjah International Book Fair. He is so energetic and always support the authors, and did encourage me as a young writer.

I thank Gopi Uncle (Gopinath Govindan, Accent Premedia), who helped me to publish my first book. He is a great inspiration and boosts me to scale new heights.

I am so thankful to my dynamic classmates, resilient teachers, and my parents, who encouraged me and just everyone out there who lent a helping hand. I once again thank everyone in my life who made it till now.

Even though this is the end of this book, here begins the adventure of my life.

With Love,

Vishnupriya Pillai

About the Author

Vishnupriya Pillai is a 10-year-old girl, born in 'God's Own Country', Kerala, India. She resides in Sharjah, United Arab Emirates and at the time of publishing this book, she is a 5th grade student in Our Own English High School, Dubai. She was the Head Girl of Primary Section in the 2020-2021 Academic Year. Her first book **'VISHNULOKA: MY WORLD OF WORDS'** was released at Sharjah International Book Fair in 2020. It was a collection of 70 poems penned by her during the lockdown days.

She spends an inordinate amount of her free time nosing through books, cooking, and catching her favourite TV shows. She is a creative and confident speaker and a passionate anchor. Being an aerobic freak, she swirls with her roller-skates.

When the pandemic turned her world upside down, she pulled out her pen and notebook and began to write down whenever interesting things happened during online classes by adding flavour and imaginations. It was there, an author was born.

9 788194 893240

Printed at Repro India Ltd.